Also by Izzy Abrahmson

The Village Life Series

The Village Twins
Winter Blessings
The Village Feasts
A Village Romance
The Council of Wise Women (Soon…)

As Mark Binder
Fictions

What Cheer!
The Groston Rules
A Dead Politician, an Undead Clam, and an Ancient Horror
Loki Ragnarok
It Ate My Sister
The Zombie Cat
The Rationalization Diet

Stories for young people

Cinderella Spinderella
The Bed Time Story Book
Kings, Wolves, Princesses and Lions
Genies, Giants and a Walrus
Classic Stories for Boys and Girls
Tall Tales, Whoppers and Lies
It was a dark and stormy night…
Stories for Peace
Transmit Joy!

A VILLAGE ROMANCE

Izzy Abrahmson

Light Publications
Providence

A Village Romance
by Izzy Abrahmson

Originally titled: **The Misadventures of Rabbi Kibbitz and Mrs.Chaipul** by Mark Binder

Design by Beth Hellman. Copy editing by Jessica Everette.

Alternate versions of "A Chanukah Surprise" and "The Lethal Latkes" are in **Winter Blessings,** and "The Lethal Latkes" in **The Village Feasts.**

Some stories originally appeared in: *The Jewish Forward, Rhode Island Jewish Herald, Hadassah Magazine, The Houston Jewish Voice, The North Shore Jewish Journal, Arizona Jewish Post, Cricket Magazine, Jewish Free Press (Calgary), Greater Phoenix Jewish News, The Jewish Journal (Youngstown), The Jewish Herald Voice, The Jewish Advocate, WholeFoods.Com, Wisconsin Jewish Chronicle.*

Softcover ISBN: 978-1-940060-53-8
ebook ISBN: 978-1-940060-32-3
audiobook ISBN: 978-1-940060-49-1
Printed in the USA • 10 9 8 7 6 5 4 3 2 1
Library of Congress Control Number: 2019947557
Light Publications
P.O. Box 2462, Providence, RI 02906
lightpublications.com • info@lightpublications.com

You know you're in love when you can't fall asleep because reality is finally better than your dreams.

–Theodor Geisel

On the edge of the Black Forest, in a part of the world that was sometimes Poland, sometimes Russia, briefly Austria, and maybe Germany, there was a small Jewish village called Chelm.

You may have heard of Chelm. Its neighbors thought the *Chelmener** were fools, and told stories that spread around the world.

The villagers themselves were ordinary people. Perhaps they knew what others said of them, perhaps not. As the wise Rabbi Kibbitz often said, "What? I can't hear you!"

In Chelm, they lived as anyone does. They worked and ate, learned and laughed. They made mistakes and, of course, they fell in love....

---

* Chelmener is the Yiddish word for the villagers of Chelm. Pronounce Chelm, Chelmener and Chaipul like you've got something caught in the back of your throat. See the glossary at the end of the book for more.

Chapter One

Why the Bride and Groom are on the Wedding Cake

Once upon a time, in the quiet village of Chelm, a man and a woman stood under the *chupah* to be married.

Jacob and Sara were very much in love. He was the best-looking young man in Chelm, and she was the most beautiful young woman. They were intelligent, kind, caring, thrifty, brave, and did I mention kind? They had courted for many many years, since they were children. In fact, they had grown up together, next-door neighbors. And now, Jacob and Sara were about to join with each other for the rest of their lives in marriage.

Surrounding the chupah, crammed into the packed-to-overflowing social hall, were so many family and friends that it seemed as if the entire village had been invited.

"A wedding," said Rabbi Kibbitz, as he stood before the couple, "a wedding is a mystical ceremony. With a few sacred words, a bond is made, and then, for the rest of eternity, the two participants' fates and lives are no longer separate, but one."

Sara looked at Jacob, and smiled. Her husband-to-be smiled back.

Rabbi Kibbitz glanced at the couple. Such a happy pair. He glowed inside.

Jacob pronounced the words of the *harey,* and gave Sara a golden band. The *ketubah* was read, and even thought the glass hadn't been broken a joyous cheer of *Mazel Tov!* rose up and nearly lifted the roof off of the social hall.

Sara's mother managed to smile through her tears, and pointed at the golden ring on her daughter's finger. Sara's father was glad that Jacob was such a wonderful boy, and of course Jacob's parents were equally pleased with their new daughter-in-law. It seemed as if happiness would never be far from this newlywed couple.

"Wait a minute!" shouted the groom over the din. "We have some vows we'd like to exchange."

Vows? Exchanging vows? The people in the social hall quieted down, for this was something they had never seen at a wedding.

"Are you sure?" Rabbi Kibbitz said. "You know, a vow is a very dangerous thing to make, because once it is made, it should never ever be broken."

"We know," the new bride said quietly, as she held her new husband's hand.

The rabbi looked at the new family, and shrugged, giving his assent. "Do you want me to say anything, or..."

"No," Jacob said, just like the authoritative businessman that his father-in-law hoped he would become.

"Thank you," added the ever-courteous Sara.

Jacob brought out a thick packet of papers, and handed half to Sara. Then, they turned to each other, and taking turns, they spoke their vows.

"I vow to you, Sara," Jacob read.

"I vow to you, Jacob," Sara answered.

"Never to break my word, never to be unfaithful, never to be far from your side.

"I vow never to be angry, to always respect you, to care for you..."

These young people, Rabbi Kibbitz thought to himself, how sweet and considerate they are to each other. I only wish that I had someone so beloved.

"I vow to always support you, to always make you happy," Sara was saying.

"I vow to stay with you forever, to keep you healthy..." Jacob intoned.

On the other hand, Rabbi Kibbitz thought, they do seem to go on and on.

The list, in fact, seemed almost endless. Rabbi Kibbitz heard Mrs. Chaipul snoring in the women's balcony.

It took Sara and Jacob more than an hour to read it all. In fact, by the time they had finished, it wasn't just Mrs. Chaipul, but many of the oldest and youngest members of the congregation were also dozing. Their vows included health, wealth, travel, children, parents, gifts, jobs, food, funeral arrangements, thank-you notes, taking out the garbage, feeding the animals: an entire system of what they promised to do for each other and with each other for the rest of their lives together!

At last, both Jacob and Sara set down their stacks of paper. The congregation (the ones who were still awake) sighed.

"All of these promises, I vow to you, Sara," Jacob said, in concluding tones.

"I vow to you also, Jacob," Sara said quietly. "We're done," she added.

"So," said Rabbi Kibbitz, "why don't you break the glass now?"

With a CRASH, Jacob stepped on the glass, symbolizing both the destruction of the Temple and the permanence of their marriage.

The sound of the shattering woke all the relations, and once again, the entire assembly cheered, shaking the roof and the walls as well.

"Mazel Tov!"

Finally, after such a long and significant delay, the happy couple took each other's hands, and, smiling, they turned as one to walk back down the aisle.

But, instead of parading proudly past their families, the new husband and wife didn't move. They stood, hand in hand, beneath the chupah, perfectly still.

"What's the matter?" said Jacob's mother.

"It's your son," said Sara's mother, "he seems to be paralyzed."

"Well, so is your daughter," snapped Jacob's mother.

And indeed, neither Jacob nor Sara were moving a muscle.

"What is it, Rabbi?" asked the two mothers. "What has happened to our children?"

Rabbi Kibbitz shook his head and frowned. He walked around Jacob and Sara, nudged them a little, waved his hand in front of their open eyes, and frowned again.

"You both have two wonderful and virtuous children," he said. "But this is something I was afraid might happen."

"What, Rabbi, what?"

Rabbi Kibbitz shrugged. "They both made so many vows to each other that they can't move for fear of breaking their promises."

Too many vows? A buzz went through the social hall. They can't move?

"Is there anything that can be done?" said Sara's mother.

The rabbi shook his head sadly. "This is something they need to work out themselves."

"In the meantime," suggested Mrs. Chaipul, the caterer, "we can go on with the party, and allow them to enjoy their wedding day as we enjoy their wedding day."

"So, why not?" said Sara's father, "It's already paid for."

And so, all the friends and relatives and villagers of Chelm celebrated. They ate and they drank. They did not lift the bride and groom in chairs, but they danced the *hora* in a circle around the statuesque couple.

When, at last, it was time to say good-bye and go home, one by one, their relatives kissed Jacob and Sara on the cheeks, and left them together alone.

From that day on, Sara and Jacob stood together in the social hall, beneath their *chupah*. Whether their marriage was happy or not, who could say? But for all those years, the relatives noted, they never once fought, and they always, always held hands.

That, my friends, is why you sometimes see the figures of a bride and groom together on top of a wedding cake. They are a symbol of Jacob and Sara's perfect unbroken marriage.

And they are also a reminder to a new husband and wife to be forgiving in the promises they make to each other.

Chapter Two

A Chanukah Surprise

It happened the year Rabbi Kibbitz lost all of his extra weight. He used to be huge, fed by Mrs. Chaipul and the rest of the sisterhood on fatty foods that he loved.

But, when the rabbi went to the railway station in Smyrna, to buy a ticket to a religious conference in London, England, the ticket master shook his head and said that he was too fat. It would take two tickets just to guarantee him a comfortable seat.

There wasn't enough money in the educational fund for two rabbis to travel.

But Rabbi Kibbitz was determined. He told Mrs. Chaipul, "Nothing but parsley, dry bread, and chicken soup with the fat skimmed until I can fit on the train."

"And so he shrunk," as Reb Stein the baker said, "from a round New Year's *challah* to a straight Sabbath *challah*."

The whole village walked all the way to Smyrna to see the rabbi off, in his huge baggy clothes.

And then, just as the train chugged out of the station, a small scrap of paper that must have been pinned to the inside to the rabbi's coat as a reminder, fluttered to the ground at the merchant, Reb Cantor's feet.

Reb Cantor and the whole village chased the train. The forgetful Rabbi was very flattered by the attention. He waved back from his window, but in a minute or two he was gone.

The villagers of Chelm gathered around Reb Cantor as he looked at the note.

"What does it say?" said Reb Gold, the cobbler.

"It's written in English," Reb Cantor said. "But it's torn, from the pin on the rabbi's coat. It says, 'Bring ——lt to the Chanukah party.'"

"Bring ——lt?" everyone said.

"Yes, ' ——lt,'" Reb Cantor said. "Part of the paper is missing."

"No it's not," said Mrs. Chaipul. "L.T. Lettuce and Tomato. For the rabbi's health salad."

"Nonsense," said Rabbi Yohon Abrahms, the schoolteacher. "There are letters missing. Obviously, the rabbi means bring geLT, for the teacher."

"Maybe it means, bring guiLT," said Reb Gold, "like on Yom Kippur."

And the debate continued.

For a whole month, while the rabbi was gone, the village prepared for the annual Chanukah party wondering what they were supposed to bring. The English dictionary in the synagogue's library was consulted until its pages were almost falling out. There was talk of little else.

"Laundry ticket! Maybe L.T. meant his laundry ticket!" said Mrs. Rosen, the washerwoman. But she checked her racks and found that the rabbi had taken all of his now-oversized clothing with him to London.

"——lt?" muttered Reb Levitzky in his sleep. "——lt!"

"What do you think the rabbi meant?" the school children asked each other. But no one knew.

The eighth night of the festival of lights arrived, and Rabbi Kibbitz still hadn't returned from England. According to the ticket master, the train had been delayed.

The party was going to have to begin without the rabbi.

One by one the people of Chelm arrived at the synagogue's social hall. And as each person came, everyone else looked to see what they had brought.

Mrs. Chaipul, of course brought her salad. Rabbi Abrahms, the schoolteacher, brought a few gold pieces, hoping that everyone else would follow his example. Reb Gold looked very depressed, and wore all black. "I haven't done anything wrong," he said, waving a finger in the air, "but I brought my guiLT."

But those were not the surprises.

Reb Levitzky wore a plaid skirt. "It's a kiLT," he said defensively.

Some fashionable women and men took the opportunity to wear their fur coats; they had brought their "peLTs." A few older men brought their best beaver hats, convinced that the rabbi meant "feLT."

Bulga, the fisherman, brought a strange toasted seafood sandwich covered with cheese. "I invented this last week," he said. "I call it a "smeLT MeLT."

From A to Z, the citizens of Chelm had mined the English dictionary and brought every conceivable variation on the mysterious letters LT. There was a bag of siLT, a sack of saLT, and even young Joel Cantor, who dressed as a SuLTan.

In fact, most of the children came in costume. They explained that they were all dressed as various "aduLTs."

The *dreidel* spun, and the eight Chanukah lights burned brightly in the huge village menorah. Everyone had a glorious time.

It was just before the younger children were about to be sent off to bed, that Mrs. Chaipul noticed the rabbi, shuffling into the back of the social hall. Without telling anyone, she escorted him to a chair and brought him a plate of her salad, a big piece of lean brisket, and a batch of newly invented non-fat potato *latkes*.

His arrival wasn't secret for long.

"Rabbi Kibbitz is here!" a shout went out. "Rabbi Kibbitz! Rabbi Kibbitz what did you mean?"

Really, the ruckus was incredible as every man, woman, and child in Chelm called out their interpretation of the rabbi's mysterious note.

"Did you really mean fiLTer?" "What about buiLT?" "SpeLT!" "No, maLT!"

Rabbi Kibbitz, who of course knew nothing of the madness his departure had caused, was puzzled until Reb Cantor (who favored "occuLT," and was wearing a magician's party cape and hat) explained the dilemma.

"What did I mean?" Rabbi Kibbitz wondered, scratching his head. "Hmm...."

"Tell us! Tell us!" the people chanted.

The rabbi raised his hand for silence. "This is a wonderful party," he said. "You've all been so inventive!

"You know, perhaps the rest of the note is still inside my coat," he said as he slid his chair back from the table where he'd been eating. He slowly stood up.

And then...

You remember that Rabbi Kibbitz had lost so much weight? Well, when he was in London, he had taken the safety pin (the very same pin that had held the note), and he had used it to take in the waist of his pants.

That pin had suspended his trousers for weeks, but after such a feast, the poor thing gave up.

So, as Rabbi Kibbitz stood up at the Chanukah party, in front of the entire village of Chelm, the safety pin popped open, and all of a sudden the famous Rabbi found himself with his trousers falling down around his ankles.

There was an embarrassed pause, and then an uproar of hysterical laughter that filled the social hall.

The learned rabbi looked down in astonishment.

"Now I remember!" he said, laughing along with everyone else. He shrugged, "I forgot to buy a beLT !"

It was truly a festival of light.

Chapter Three

Open for Business

There are no strangers in Chelm. Nearly every one who lives there was born there. The rest arrive because of marriage. After all, you can only havc so many generations living in the same village before someone accidentally marries a cousin. In any case, whenever someone new settled in Chelm, it was always because of a matrimonial contract.

Except Mrs. Chaipul.

Years ago, when Mrs. Chaipul first arrived in Chelm it was unexpected, unannounced, and, as far as anyone could tell, out of thin air. She hadn't traveled with a peddler or a trader or a caravan of Gypsies. None of the farmers who kept careful watch on the road from Smyrna saw this lone elderly woman making her way into the village.

The first person who met her was Reb Cantor's maid servant, Ramunya.

It was just after dawn, when the door to the merchant's house opened. Ramunya was on her way to get water from the village well when she nearly tripped over the old woman sitting on a sack on the doorstep.

"Ahh!" shouted the startled maid. "Who are you? What do you want?"

"I'm Mrs. Chaipul. I would like to speak with Reb Cantor about a property."

"Property shmoperty. It's not even six in the morning! Reb Cantor is never awake before noon. Even then, I doubt if he'll see you."

Off the girl went.

Mrs. Chaipul blinked. "I'll wait."

When the girl returned, Mrs. Chaipul rose and helped her by opening the door. "I think your bread is burning."

"What do you know?" Then, Ramunya sniffed the air, smelled the smoke, and ran, spilling water all over the front hallway.

Mrs. Chaipul sighed, opened her sack, took out two towels, and began wiping up the puddle in the merchant's front hall.

A minute later, the girl was back, her eyes filled with tears. "It's ruined!" she cried. "The bread is completely ruined. I'll be fired. I'll be turned out into the streets, and then I'll die of starvation and cold."

"Nonsense," said the old woman. "May I show you a trick?"

The hopeless young girl nodded. She led Mrs. Chaipul into the kitchen where two loaves sat smoking on a cooling rack.

The breads were charred black, but Mrs. Chaipul simply took a long sharp knife and cut off all the burned parts. "There! Feed these crumbs to the birds."

"Reb Cantor will accuse me of stealing crusts of bread," sobbed the girl. "They'll throw me in jail and feed me nothing but bread and water until I see visions."

Mrs. Chaipul frowned. "Are you sure you want to work for this family?"

"Yes," nodded the girl. "They are wonderful and sweet and generous."

"Fine," Mrs. Chaipul said. "Simply tell them that you made them a special recipe of crustless bread."

The girl nodded, thanked Mrs. Chaipul, and went about her chores, quite forgetting the old lady sitting in the corner.

It was half past noon when the kitchen door opened and a fat man peeked in.

"You?" he demanded.

"Me?" Mrs. Chaipul asked.

"Did you give my servant girl a special recipe for crustless bread?"

"It depends," answered Mrs. Chaipul.

"On what does it depend?"

"Are you going to beat her, or fire her, or have her thrown into jail?"

The man tilted his head back and laughed. "What nonsense! Ramunya is new. She's only been here for seven years. Her mother was my wife's mother's second cousin. She's clumsy, she's slow, and she's obviously rude to guests, but she's family. When she's old enough, I'll help her find a good husband..."

"Yes, yes," Mrs. Chaipul interrupted. "I taught her the recipe."

"Well, thank you! It's wonderful. My daughter, Rivka, she refused to eat bread that had crusts. We didn't know what to do. Now we have crustless bread, and she ate an entire loaf!"

Mrs. Chaipul looked thoughtful. "Couldn't you simply cut the crusts off an ordinary bread?"

The man looked stunned. "Two brilliant ideas! How can I help you?"

At last, the opportunity she'd been waiting for. The old woman's face broadened into a smile. "My name is Chanah Chaipul, and I want to buy a property from you."

"Why don't we talk over breakfast?"

"I'm sorry," Mrs. Chaipul shook her head, "but I never eat breakfast after noon."

"But I never talk business until after I eat," the merchant said, patting his belly.

"Perhaps I could have lunch?" Mrs. Chaipul suggested.

"Three brilliant ideas in one day! My dear lady, you are a miracle."

During the meal, Mrs. Chaipul explained that she wanted to buy an old and deserted stable near the village square and convert it into a restaurant. Reb Cantor tried to persuade her that Chelm was too small for a restaurant, and that renting was a better option than buying.

After lunch, they went over to inspect the building, and by dinner time the deal was concluded. Mrs. Chaipul paid cash, which she explained, she had inherited from her dead husband.

"Sam always put money away for a rainy day," she said, counting the rubles into Reb Cantor's hand. "It snowed a lot, but it never rained."

After such an unexpected windfall, Reb Cantor invited Mrs. Chaipul to supper, but she gracefully declined.

"I have too much work to do. I must get started immediately."

He shook his head and sighed as he watched the old woman tug the squeaky stable door shut. She was a strange one to be sure, and he wished her the best.

Others in Chelm were not so kind.

"Chelm needs a restaurant like a horse needs wheels," said one gossip.

"I hear she killed her first six husbands," answered a second.

"Where did you hear such a thing?" asked a third.

"Who can remember?"

Mrs. Chaipul ignored them all. She put a new roof on the stable by herself, and she hired local craftsmen to tear down walls, repair plaster, and build counters, tables, and a kitchen.

"She spends money like it's going out of style."

"She ought to save some for a rainy day."

While the restaurant was still under construction, Mrs. Chaipul began to develop a reputation as a healer. When one of the workers slipped and sawed off a finger, Mrs. Chaipul applied a poultice and then sewed it back on, "As good as new!" When Ramunya was sick for a week, she visited the Cantor house, gave her a potion, and the girl was back on her feet the next morning.

Now the busybodies really had something to talk about.

"I think she's a witch."

"What nonsense."

"Just watch. She'll poison us all!"

When the "Grand Opening" sign went up in front of the so-called restaurant, a delegation went to Rabbi Kibbitz with a laundry list of complaints.

The rabbi stared at the villagers crowded into his office. He read the list.

"Murder. Witchcraft. Poisonings?" He looked solemn. "These are serious charges. Have you any proof? No? Then stop gossiping!"

No one said a word. One by one they all left, embarrassed.

Still, the rabbi was a prudent man. He decided it was time to pay a visit.

It was late in the afternoon when he arrived at the stable. The old and decrepit building with a broken roof and mud-stained walls was now a beautifully whitewashed restaurant, with big windows, clean tables, and comfortable-looking chairs.

He opened the door, and a little bell jingled.

"Have a seat," said a voice. "I'll be right with you."

Rabbi Kibbitz looked around. The restaurant was empty. There were five tables with four chairs each, and a long counter with six stools. He chose the table farthest from the door and sat. The chair was very comfortable. He sighed. The room was cozy. And the smell... It was heavenly. Something was cooking, something rich and warm and almost certainly delicious.

A moment later, an elderly but handsome woman appeared at his side with a pad of paper.

"Good afternoon, Rebbe," she said. "You're my first customer. Would you like some coffee or tea?"

He hadn't really thought about it. "Tea would be nice."

Then, before he knew it, he was sipping on a hot cup of tea, sweetened with honey.

"This is good," he said. "It makes a nice break in the middle of the day."

Mrs. Chaipul smiled, as if she already knew.

Although Rabbi Kibbitz invited her to join him, she refused. He was nice looking, and seemed kindly, but people would talk.

"I understand that the villagers have their suspicions," she said, standing behind the counter as she polished silverware. "It's to be expected. I'm sure they'll forget everything once they find out that their first meal is free.

Speaking of which, I happen to have a bit of brisket. Would you like to try some?"

Rabbi Kibbitz never hesitated when offered a free meal. An instant later, she brought a plate piled high with brisket, potatoes, cabbage, and a chunk of brown bread. He sniffed, smiled, and was about to take a bite when a thought crossed his mind.

"It's not poisoned, is it?"

Instantly, Mrs. Chaipul's smile vanished. "Already you're criticizing my cooking? You haven't even tasted it. I'd offer you a refund, but you haven't even paid me. Get out!"

"No no no," the rabbi said quickly. "I apologize. I meant to ask if it was kosher. The wrong word slipped out."

She frowned. "Of course it's kosher. What else would it be?"

"Well," the rabbi reasoned softly to himself, "if it's kosher then it can't be poisoned..."

He lifted his fork to his mouth and...

It was delicious!

"Bis is goob," he said, grinning and chewing loudly.

Mrs. Chaipul allowed her smile to return.

When the rabbi was finished, he dabbed the corners of his mouth with his napkin, pushed his chair back, and sighed.

"I wish I could eat like this every day."

"Why not?"

He smiled at the woman behind the counter. She had good shoulders and a firm gaze. "Well, I doubt I could afford it."

"You have to eat. Don't the villagers pay you a salary?"

"Yes, yes, but Chelm is a small and poor village. It can't afford such extravagance."

"Extravagance? Nonsense!" Mrs. Chaipul snorted. Now she took off her apron and sat down at his table with a piece of paper and a pencil. In five minutes, the rabbi had a meal plan that could actually save him money!

"You'll go broke with prices like this. And free food also?"

"Rabbi Kibbitz," Mrs. Chaipul said. "May I call you Rabbi Kibbitz?"

"Of course, that's my name."

"Rabbi Kibbitz, because I run a restaurant, I'll never starve. I sleep upstairs, and the stove keeps the whole building warm."

"But won't you need a man to help?"

She snorted. "Nonsense! I lived with my husband, may he rest in peace, for twenty-five years. I cooked, and cleaned, and raised six children, and sent them off into the world. Did he help with that? Well, a little. But now they're all gone, off and about, and he's gone for good. So here I am. Would you like some more tea? Perhaps a little dessert?"

"Dessert?" Rabbi Kibbitz's face fell. He hadn't saved any room. "I don't think it will fit."

"Nonsense... Try this."

She slid a piece of walnut strudel in front of the rabbi, who attacked it like a hungry child.

The next day Mrs. Chaipul's restaurant was filled to over-flowing. Every one in Chelm wanted their free meal, and after they'd tasted her briskets, her chicken, her stews, and most especially her desserts, they were customers for life.

A year quickly came and went, and one morning Reb Cantor was sitting at the counter sipping on his fifth cup of tea. He was by now a regular, eating at ten in the morning because Mrs. Chaipul refused to serve him breakfast any later.

"You've done well for yourself, Chanah," he told her.

She smiled and nodded.

"But you've forgotten one thing."

"What's that?"

"When are you going to give your restaurant a name?"

"How many other restaurants are there in Chelm?"

The other morning regulars, Reb Gold, Reb Stein, and Rabbi Kibbitz laughed.

"My restaurant needs a name?" Mrs. Chaipul muttered. "Nonsense."

Then she smiled and whispered it again, "Nonsense." It was a good name for a restaurant, but she kept it to herself.

Chapter Four

The Village Workout

Who in Chelm is stronger, the men or the women?

It depends on who you ask.

One day, Mrs. Rosen saw a notice on the bulletin board in the back of Mrs. Chaipul's restaurant. It read, "Have you lost your energy? Does picking up after the *kinder* day in and day out make you tired? Wouldn't you like to feel alive again?"

Mrs. Rosen nodded her head. Yes, yes, yes, she thought. So, what do I do about it?

"Come to an exercise class," the sign answered. "Starts Thursday morning in the Synagogue's social hall."

No, that was impossible. Thursday was cleaning day. In fact, her whole week was full. She took in laundry on Mondays and Wednesdays. Tuesdays were for household repairs. Fridays, of course, were devoted to Shabbas preparations, and Sundays she caught up on anything she hadn't finished from the week before. In between, she cared for the children, went shopping, cooked, and cleaned up from meals. Not to mention holidays, holy days, and festivals. No, whatever an exercise class was, it was just plain foolishness. So, she promptly forgot all about it... until Thursday morning.

Mrs. Rosen was on her knees, scrubbing the kitchen floor, when there was an unexpected knocking at her door. She dropped the brush into its bucket, got up, and opened the door.

Standing outside was Mrs. Chaipul, the widow who owned Chelm's only restaurant. "Aren't you coming to the exercise class?"

"My kitchen floor is wet," said Mrs. Rosen. She noticed a dozen more women of Chelm standing behind Mrs. Chaipul, laughing and chattering.

"The floor will dry," said Mrs. Chaipul. "You have to come. The instructor has traveled all the way from Minsk to teach us. We want her to think well of Chelm, don't we?"

"Minsk?" Mrs. Rosen said. "She traveled all that way by herself?"

"She walked," Mrs. Chaipul said. "She says she'll be staying in Chelm for a month, and teaching every morning, except Shabbas. She says that exercise is the best thing for a woman to do for herself, aside from the *mitzvah* of trying to start a family of course." Mrs. Chaipul winked, and Mrs. Rosen blushed.

The children were at school, her husband was at work in the fields, and who would know except her poor dead mother (rest her soul) if the floor was not washed spotless this once?

"I'll come!"

• • •

That evening, Reb Rosen was surprised to find his children running around outside the house like a pack of wild animals and his wife asleep with her head on the kitchen table, a half-peeled potato in her hand.

"Deborah," he said, "is something the matter? Are you ill?"

"Martin," she smiled through bleary eyes. "I've never felt better." She hoisted herself up from the table with a groan, and stumbled off into the bedroom where she promptly fell asleep.

Reb Rosen looked at the half-peeled potato and wondered how he might turn that into a meal.

Every morning for the next four weeks, Mrs. Rosen made her way to the social hall for the exercise class. At first it was difficult. For one thing, she *shvitzed* like a horse. She tripped and fell. Her very bones were sore.

If this is good for me, she thought, a long stay in a Russian prison would do me wonders.

Then she noticed that every other woman in Chelm was struggling and sweating as much as she. By the end of the third week, she was feeling better. True the laundry wasn't all done, the back of the stove had a bit of dust on it, and dinners were nearly always late. But she found that she could walk all the way to and from market in Smyrna without stopping once. And when she finally did move the stove to clean behind it, the task was almost effortless.

"This is wonderful!" she panted to Mrs. Chaipul during one class. It was foolishness to be sure. There she was, a grown woman, running around the social hall flapping her arms like a bloated pigeon trying to take off. "I love this!"

Mrs. Chaipul, who was a bit older, just nodded her head and coughed.

Peeking in through the social hall's door, Reb Rosen watched the women's absurd behavior and shook his head sadly. For almost a month he had seen his wife's condition deteriorate. At first she was simply exhausted. Meals were irregular, and the laundry smelled odd. Then the food began to change. Instead of meat and potatoes, or a nice chicken with dumplings for dinner, he was served plates of leaves and strange green plants. His wife called it, "salad and vegetables." It looked like mulch. He asked around and learned that the story was the same throughout the village of Chelm. Now he knew why. The women had fallen under the influence of a witch. He closed the door quietly, walked down the hall, and knocked on the door to the rabbi's study.

"Our wives," said Reb Rosen when the rabbi finally looked up from his reading, "are bewitched. They are acting like madwomen and giving us food better fit for cows or goats."

"I know," Rabbi Kibbitz nodded. "Mrs. Chaipul used to put lots of chicken or cheese in her health salad. No more. Now, it's like eating grass. But I do think Mrs. Chaipul is looking rather nice and *svelte*, don't you?"

"What? You know about this?" Reb Rosen was shocked. "You're permitting this?"

"The instructor walked all the way from Minsk," the rabbi said. "What could I say? But, she is leaving next week. Then it will be over."

"By next week I'll be dead of starvation," said Reb Rosen, "and my wife will be nothing but bones! Already when I hug her I can touch my own elbows. Are you sure that this instructor is not a witch?"

"Yes." Rabbi Kibbitz nodded his head and returned to his studies.

For Reb Rosen and all the other married men of Chelm, the next week passed as quickly as a garden slug making its way across the road. No matter how many "vegetables" they ate, hunger gnawed at their bellies. Their pants grew baggy, and they had to tie their belts tighter. And in the mornings, when they woke, they found their ribs and arms bruised from lying beside their once *zaftig* brides.

The evening after the exercise instructor finally left Chelm for Smyrna, Reb Rosen (and every other husband of Chelm) lifted his glass in thanks for the deliverance. Life had returned to normal. The floors were spotless, the clothing smelled clean, and once again the Sabbath potatoes tasted rich with *schmaltz*.

Reb Rosen patted his comfortable belly and looked around to offer his compliments to his beloved.

He found that she had gone to bed early, and that her pillow was wet with tears.

This will pass, he thought. Soon she will forget about the witch's "exercise" and return to her days of plump joy.

But the gloom did not pass, and as the days turned into weeks, Mrs. Rosen (and many other wives of Chelm) grew fatter, but no happier.

At last, Reb Rosen returned to the rabbi's study. "The women need a class," he said to the rabbi. "An exercise class."

"I know," said Rabbi Kibbitz. "But the instructor has already left Smyrna. I already asked. No one there knows where she has gone."

"I have an idea," Reb Rosen said.

That evening, after a joyless dinner, Reb Rosen put his hand on his wife's shoulder.

"Deborah," he asked, "would you like to do another exercise class?"

Her eyes brightened in a way he hadn't seen for so long. She nodded silently.

"Do you think?" he said. "Do you think you might be able to lead the class by yourself? The teacher is gone, but perhaps you remember what you learned..." His voice trailed off.

"Are you sure?" she said.

He nodded.

"I would like that," she said. "But I thought you didn't approve of my exercise."

Reb Rosen shrugged. "How can I be happy when you are not? But I have one request. Can't we please have some meat at dinner? Salad is all right for goats, but..."

He didn't have a chance to finish. Mrs. Rosen gave her husband a hug so tight he winced, and the very next day exercise classes resumed.

Who in Chelm is stronger, the men or the women?

It all depends on who you ask.

Chapter Five

What's In A Name?

Speaking of weddings...

It was another beautiful wedding. Isaac Finkle had finally managed to marry Leah Goodman. Now they were taking a moment that had become traditional in Chelm to stop by the still spellbound figures of Jacob and Sara to ask for their blessings. And as always, the immobile bride and groom beamed their silent good wishes.

Mrs. Chaipul, a widow, stood at the back of the Social Hall, and watched the celebration with silent pleasure. As the owner and operator of Chelm's sole kosher restaurant, the village's chief caterer, and the best wedding planner within four day's ride, she was pleased with the results. The food was delicious, none of the flowers were wilting, and even after the wine had been poured the band was still playing on key.

"You do wonderful work, Mrs. Chaipul," Rabbi Kibbitz said, startling the poor woman.

"Thank you Rabbi." She smiled from ear to ear.

"I wonder, " the rabbi continued, "who could possibly do such a wonderful job planning the meal for our wedding?"

"Our wedding?" Mrs. Chaipul gave him a curious look.

"Yes," Rabbi Kibbitz nodded, shyly. "If you'll have me?"

"You know," Mrs. Chaipul said, "you really must ask me more directly. A woman is apt to misunderstand such questions."

"Hmm," the rabbi nodded, and stroked his long beard. "All right. So, will you marry me?"

"You?" Mrs. Chaipul looked skeptical. Then she shrugged. "Why not?"

"Was that a yes?" Rabbi Kibbitz asked. "You know, men are apt to misunderstand such answers."

"Yes," Mrs. Chaipul nodded. She looked him in the eyes. Her grin, which had been large before, grew as wide as a brisket.

"Ahh!" The rabbi's eyes twinkled happily. "But you still have not answered my first question. Who will plan our wedding?"

"You must be kidding?" said Mrs. Chaipul. She reached into her voluminous handbag, and pulled out a scroll of tightly rolled parchment an inch thick, which if it were unfurled would have been at least thirty feet long. "I have it all worked out already."

The rabbi began chuckling. Mrs. Chaipul joined in, and together they laughed very loudly.

The villagers whispered and stared.

• • •

It took less than six months for Mrs. Chaipul to finish all her planning and organization for their wedding. It took another three months after that for the last minute details to be worked out. There was so much to do, from embroidering the right fabric for the *chupah*, to arranging with Reb Stein for a certain type of challah, to convincing Reb Cantor to track down and purchase a pair of snow white beeswax candles imported from Palestine.

At last, though Rabbi Kibbitz had been half sure it would never come, the happy day arrived.

It was a gorgeous day for an outdoor ceremony. Everyone joked that the Rabbi had put in a good word with The Almighty. Rabbi Yohon Abrahms, the head of the *yeshiva* officiated, and the entire village of Chelm, as well as many important officials from surrounding, communities attended.

When Rabbi Kibbitz broke the glass that sealed the bond, a joyful shout of "Mazel Tov!" arose that was heard all the way to Jerusalem.

On the platform, which had been built in the village square, Rabbi Kibbitz stood before his new bride, about to kiss her for the first time on the lips.†

"So, Rebbitzen Kibbitz," he said, holding her hands gently, "we're married at last!" His smiling cheeks glowed beneath his snow white beard.

"Wait a moment!" the bride said, suddenly turning her cheek. She jerked one hand free of her husband's grip and held a finger upraised in front of his lips. "What did you call me?"

"Rebbitzen Kibbitz," the rabbi said. Then he timidly added, "Isn't that all right?"

"Absolutely not." Now the bride looked angry. "I have been Mrs. Chaipul for decades. You don't expect me to change now?"

"But," said Rabbi Yohon Abrahms, "now you're the rabbi's wife..."

"You stay out of this young fellow." The bride's angry finger pointed at the officiating rabbi, who backed away and nearly fell off the platform.

---

† The thought of two old people kissing publicly may be as shocking to you as it was to some of the younger children in Chelm, but let's not get ahead of ourselves.

The whole village fell eagerly silent. It wasn't often you got a chance to see two newlyweds engage in their first married fight, and under the chupah no less.

"What do you expect me to do as Rebbitzen?" the bride said. "Stay at home and make you dinner?"

"That would be nice," Rabbi Kibbitz shrugged. The bride snorted loudly. "I thought," he continued, "that you would become the head of the sisterhood."

"I already am the head of the sisterhood," she said in dismay. "Do you really want me to close the restaurant?"

There was a gasp from the villagers and the visitors. Mrs. Chaipul's restaurant was famous for a hundred miles.

"Close the restaurant?" The eldest rabbi of Chelm looked dismayed. "I hadn't thought of that."

The whole village of Chelm held its breath. No! Not the restaurant. The nearest other kosher restaurant was in Smyrna, half a day's ride away.

"No." Rabbi Kibbitz shook his head firmly. "No. You don't have to close the restaurant, unless you want to."

A sigh of relief was breathed by every man, woman, and child.

"But I feel uncomfortable," the groom continued, "for you to be married to me with another man's name."

"Nonsense." The bride gently touched the groom's elbow. "Do you remember what my late husband's name was?"

Rabbi Kibbitz nodded. "How could I forget? You told me his name was Sam."

"Sam," the bride said, nodding. "Sam Klammerdinger. Oy, what a name. As soon as he passed away, I took my mother's mother's name back."

"I didn't know that," Rabbi Kibbitz said, his face brightening slightly.

"Why should I tell anyone?" the bride said, "Not that I didn't love Sam while he was alive, but who wants to be called Mrs. Klammerdinger?"

"So, you want to be called Rebbitzen Chaipul?" Rabbi Kibbitz said.

"No. No," the bride insisted firmly. "Call me Mrs. Chaipul. I'll be married to you, but I'm not working for you."

"Mrs. Chaipul?" Rabbi Kibbitz repeated, still looking puzzled.

"But won't that be confusing," interrupted Rabbi Yohon Abrahms. "What about the children?"

Both the bride and the groom gave the young rabbi a sarcastic look. As two of the village's most respected citizens, they were not exactly spring chickens.

"When I get pregnant," the bride said, patting Rabbi Abrahms gently on the top of his head, "we'll work it out."

"Well," Rabbi Yohon Abrahms agreed with a shrug, "if it works for you..."

"Wait!" Rabbi Kibbitz crossed his arms. Now he was angry. "I can't call you Mrs. Chaipul. You're my wife? What will I call you?"

"You?" His bride looked him straight in the eyes and said softly, "You will call me Chanah."

With that, the rabbi's anger and fear melted away.

They kissed under the chupah, alone together, surrounded by exuberant cheers, and the sound of a *klezmer* band playing their love with joy.

Chapter Six

New Beginnings

"Good morning, Rabbi."

Rabbi Kibbitz of Chelm looked up from behind his study table to see his old friend, Rabbi Sarnoff of Smyrna.

"I like to visit with you before *Rosh Hashanah*," Rabbi Sarnoff said, "because after the holy days start, as you know, it's madness."

Rabbi Kibbitz smiled and nodded his agreement. He held up a finger that said, wait a moment, and reached for a small box beside a huge pile of books...

Just then, Reb Cantor the merchant burst into the rabbi's study.

"Rabbi, I've got a problem," Reb Cantor said breathlessly. Then he noticed Rabbi Sarnoff. "Oh, hello, Rabbi. I hope I'm not interrupting, but I've got this problem. It's burning. It has been eating away at my insides like acid. I can't contain it for another minute."

"Is it about your business?" Rabbi Sarnoff asked. Reb Cantor was well known in Smyrna as a middleman, importer, and exporter. "Is something wrong with your business?"

"No," said Reb Cantor. "Just the opposite. And that's the problem. Business is wonderful. I have never had such a good summer. Everything is going smoothly. Couldn't be better. It's driving me absolutely crazy!"

Rabbi Kibbitz looked puzzled.

"I'm not sure I understand either," said Rabbi Sarnoff. "You're upset because your business is doing well?"

"Exactly." Reb Cantor nodded his head vigorously. "I'm making money hand over foot. It's like a bountiful harvest. A reward for so many years of hard work and suffering."

"So," Rabbi Sarnoff asked, "what's the problem?"

"Ah, the problem." Reb Cantor lowered his voice. He started slowly but quickly began to pick up steam and volume. "You know the saying, 'The new year brings new beginnings?' New beginnings are change. It's like the *Torah* says, seven years of feast and then seven years of famine. I am on top of the world right now.

Everything is so wonderful. I feel as if there is no place for me to go but down. It's making me crazy!"

Exhausted, Reb Cantor dropped into a chair. Both he and Rabbi Sarnoff looked toward Rabbi Kibbitz. The room fell silent.

The old man stroked his long white beard. He twirled his curls around his fingers. He reached for the small black box beside the pile of books and...

"Of course!" Reb Cantor said. "The New Year is a new beginning. It's an opportunity to expand, to grow beyond what I have ever thought possible. Of course there should be worries at a time like this. I'd be crazy not to worry. I'm not at the top of the world, not yet, just a small hill. And I've been looking down that hill thinking, it's such a long way to fall. Now, I will turn around and see the mountain in front of me, and think, what a long way to climb! How far I have yet to go."

Reb Cantor stood. He shook Rabbi Sarnoff's hand. "Sorry for interrupting." He turned to Rabbi Kibbitz. "Rabbi, you are indeed a wise man. I shall be making a sizable donation this year, but next year it will be even more!"

Then, with a great grin on his face, Reb Cantor left as quickly as he had come.

"Well," said Rabbi Sarnoff.

Once again, Rabbi Kibbitz reached for the black box and…

There was a knock. "Rabbi?" A head peeked in, followed by the rest of the body. It was Reb Stern, the rag man. Where Reb Cantor was fat and well dressed, Reb Stern was thin and his clothes were nearly transparent. And the smell? It reminded Rabbi Kibbitz of the odor that filled the shul as soon as the first cabbage harvest was cooked and eaten. Reb Stern needed a bath. Still, he was a villager of Chelm and welcome in the rabbi's study.

"Begging your pardon," Reb Stern coughed, "but I have been feeling poorly. My horse died not long ago, and I have had to pull my wagon through all the mud and ruts from the rains."

Rabbi Kibbitz gestured to the chair so recently abandoned by Reb Cantor. Reb Stern sat stiffly.

"My wife is ill," Reb Stern continued. "My sons have gone off and I haven't heard from them in months. And do you know what else? The roof of my house is leaking and my ladder is broken. I don't even know if I can afford a challah for our Rosh Hashanah dinner." He looked glumly at his shoes, which were more hole than leather. Rabbi Sarnoff saw the poor man's toes wiggling nervously.

Both Reb Stern and Rabbi Sarnoff looked toward Rabbi Kibbitz. The room fell silent.

The wise old man stroked his long white beard. He twirled his curls around his fingers. Again he reached for the small black box beside the pile of books and...

"Of course, the new year brings new beginnings," Reb Stern said, nodding thoughtfully. "It can always get worse, but it might get better as well. I have been treating my problems as if I am the only man in the world with difficulties. There are many even less fortunate than I. And perhaps someone who is more fortunate will lend me a ladder, so I can fix the roof at last. Then when we do save a few coppers for a challah, we will be dry when we eat it. Then perhaps my wife will get better, and maybe my sons will come home with a horse. Or even better, a mule. They eat less and pull more. Who needs to go as fast as a horse? Not I. While pulling my cart I have enjoyed watching the countryside creep past. It would be nice to ride, but I am a fortunate man. I have lived a good life. And as you said, the new year brings new beginnings."

Reb Stern stood with a small smile beginning to grow on his face and said, "I am sorry for interrupting your conversation."

Rabbi Sarnoff reached into his pocket and gave Reb Stern a small silver piece. "Not charity," Rabbi Sarnoff said, "but a gift. Or if you won't take a gift, an investment in the future of an honest man."

Reb Stern nodded thoughtfully, thanked Rabbi Sarnoff, pocketed the coin, and turned to Rabbi Kibbitz.

"Once again, Rabbi Kibbitz," Reb Stern began, "you have shown that you are indeed the wisest man in Chelm."

Rabbi Kibbitz smiled and shrugged as Reb Stern left the room with more than a little bounce in his step.

"Amazing," Rabbi Sarnoff said. "Such problems you have in Chelm. I was stumped. Yet, you knew exactly what to say to both of them..."

This time, Rabbi Kibbitz didn't wait a moment. He quickly snatched up the small black box beside the huge pile of books. He pried the lid open, removed a set of false teeth, and popped them into his mouth.

"I can't say a thing without my teeth in," Rabbi Kibbitz said. Then the old man grinned.

Rabbi Sarnoff threw his head back, and together they both laughed.

It was indeed a good year.

Chapter Seven

The Lethal Latkes

The villagers of Chelm dreaded Chanukah. It wasn't the holiday itself. They loved lighting the candles, spinning the dreidel, and retelling the stories of the Maccabees and the miracle of the lights. All in all, Chanukah was a wonderful festival, except for one thing: Mrs. Chaipul's *latkes*, which were served in great abundance at the village's Chanukah party.

Mrs. Chaipul's latkes were not good. They were really not good. It wasn't that they were too greasy (which they were) or that they were too heavy (which they were) or even that they were burned (which they almost always were), it was the smell. There was something slightly sickening about the smell of Mrs. Chaipul's latkes. Not repulsive like a dirty stable, or a fish that's been left out too long. More nauseating and unsettling, as if there was something dead and forgotten in the cellar, and you can't quite put your finger on what it was and where to find it so you can clean it up.

The problem was that Mrs. Chaipul owned the only restaurant in Chelm. Other than her latkes, her food was fine. In fact, in her restaurant, her food was delicious. However, whenever she left her own kitchen, and cooked for the multitudes for the Chanukah party at the shul's social hall... It was a disaster. Especially those latkes.

But now that Mrs. Chaipul had recently married Rabbi Kibbitz, (keeping her own maiden name, as you know,) some of the villagers decided that perhaps it was time to broach the subject.

A few days before Chanukah, the rabbi heard a knock on the door of his study. He looked up from his reading and saw four of the village's finest citizens, standing nervously with their hats in their hands. There was Reb Rosen, the farmer, Rabbi Abrahms, the school teacher, Reb Cantor, the merchant, and Reb Stein, the baker.

Rabbi Kibbitz welcomed them in.

In a matter of minutes, the story was presented. As much as they loved Mrs. Chaipul, Reb Cantor said, her latkes made everyone sick. Her famous matzah balls were as heavy as lead, but at least they were still delicious.‡ No one looked forward to nibbling on her latkes.

"And worst of all," added Reb Stein, "she always piles the plate so high! You don't want to offend her by not eating them all, but for the next three days... nothing tastes good."

The rabbi nodded his head wisely. He knew exactly what they were talking about. Over the years he had developed a trick of hiding several of the latkes in his pockets and then slipping out the back door to feed them to a goat. And sometimes even the goat got sick. But he shrugged, "What do you suggest?"

"Well," said Rabbi Abrahms, "you're married to her. You could bring it up."

"Tactfully, of course," said Reb Rosen.

"You're right," the rabbi agreed, shaking their hands. "There is nothing that a husband and wife should not be able to talk about."

He was wrong.

That evening, Rabbi Kibbitz brought up the subject, and his wife, Mrs. Chaipul, slammed the door in his face. Literally. She wouldn't let him into their bedroom. He had to spend the night curled up underneath the kitchen table, shivering with cold.

---

‡ See the next chapter, "Mrs. Chaipul's Lead Sinker Matzah Balls."

"What have I done?" the rabbi moaned that night, and for the next seven evenings. "Is my marriage ruined? Who can the rabbi talk with when he has problems?"

The night of the Chanukah party arrived. Rabbi Kibbitz, who by now was stiff and exhausted, was not at all interested in attending. After the evening prayers, he went for a long walk. He was seriously considering skipping the whole party and crawling into bed for a nap, until his wife came home and kicked him out. Still, he was the village rabbi, and his place was with his congregation.

So, he stood in front of the doors to the social hall, and steeled himself for the ordeal that was to come. You see, the rabbi himself felt nauseated just from the smell of his wife's latkes. They always reminded him of the embarrassing odors that wafted from his aunt's wet lips when he was a child.

Finally, he opened the door, stepped inside, and held his breath for as long as possible. He walked through the room quickly, smiling and shaking hands.

At last, gasping and feeling faint, he was forced to inhale deeply.

What was this? He breathed again. He didn't feel sick. He sniffed the air. There was something good smelling here. His nose twitched like a bunny's. Not sickening at all, but sweet and delicious. He turned to the stove where the latkes were always made, and much to his surprise saw Deborah and Esther Rosen, the farmer's wife and eldest unmarried daughter, laughing and frying latkes as if they had done so forever. There was a line for the latkes, and the rabbi noticed that as soon as the other villagers got their plates filled, they scurried to the back of the line, and ate standing up while they waited for more.

"Good job!" said Rabbi Abrahms, patting the senior rabbi on the back.

"Best latkes ever," agreed Reb Cantor.

"Come," said Reb Rosen, taking the rabbi by the arms and leading him to the front of the line. "You deserve to eat some of these."

Mrs. Rosen piled the rabbi's plate high with the most perfect golden brown latkes he had ever seen. They were thin and crisp and delicate with just a light sheen of oil.

Everyone watched as he cut into them, and lifted the fork to his mouth. From this close, they smelled even better than they had at the door. Like the warm sun of summer made alive once again in the midst of winter.

Just as Rabbi Kibbitz was about to close his mouth around the latkes, he saw his wife watching him from across the room. Her face was neutral, expressionless.

The rabbi bit in, and sighed as the latkes melted deliciously in his mouth.

"Very good," he smiled. Mrs. Rosen hugged her daughter. "Still," he continued, "I like my wife's latkes better."

There was a moment's astonished silence, and then all at once the social hall filled with laughter at the rabbi's wonderful joke.

No one noticed when the rabbi set his plate down unfinished and sneaked out. He walked back to his house, where he crawled into bed for a nap.

He awoke when he heard the front door shut. Grumbling, the rabbi began to get himself ready to sleep under the kitchen table.

"Stay. Don't get up," said Mrs. Chaipul putting a hand on her husband's arm. "I know Deborah's latkes are better than mine. I asked her for the recipe, and tomorrow she's going to show me. Still, it was sweet of you to say that you liked mine best." Then she kissed her husband on the cheek.

"But I do," said the rabbi.

Mrs. Chaipul laughed and closed her eyes.

The funny thing was, Rabbi Kibbitz thought, he really did like his wife's latkes better. True, they tasted awful and smelled worse, but they had been made with love. Her love. And for him that was the most delicious flavor in the world.

Chapter Eight

Mrs. Chaipul's Lead Sinker Matzah Balls

Mrs. Chaipul is actually a wonderful cook. When you run the only kosher restaurant in the village of Chelm, you have to be. Her *kugel* is incredible; her *kreplach* are tender and moist; her corned beef and cabbage melts in your mouth; her roasted potatoes are hot and crisp; and her split pea soup is so rich and robust, you'd swear it was *treif.* Even her potato latkes, which once were the scourge of Chanukah, have improved greatly over the past few years.

But her lead sinker matzah balls are never going to change. This is the story of those matzah balls, and how they saved the village of Chelm.

Back when Mrs. Chaipul came to Chelm, she brought her matzah ball recipe with her. It had been in her family for generations, passed down in secret from mother to daughter.

In the Chaipul family, jaw-breaking matzah balls were an immutable tradition, like plucking a chicken on the first day of spring. Every year, the men in the family joked that the secret was building construction mortar. The women greeted this comment with stony silence. At one Seder, Mrs. Chaipul's grandfather Moishe Chaipul argued for six hours that if the pyramids had been built from Chaipul *knaidlach*, then they would still be standing. Never mind the fact that his son-in-law, Sam Klammerdinger,[§] tried to convince the Chaipuls that the pyramids were in fact still standing.

In Chelm, the villagers' first taste of the Chaipul knaidel was the second year after she had opened the restaurant. The first year, Mrs. Chaipul was too busy to clean and make the facility kosher for Passover, so she shut down and arranged for a *goyishe* intermediary to buy the restaurant for the eight-day festival.

During that first Passover in Chelm, Mrs. Chaipul was invited to eat at the house of every villager. After all, with her shop closed, who was going to feed her?

Naturally she accepted Shoshana Cantor's invitation. Who wouldn't? Wasn't Reb Cantor

§ Mrs. Chaipul's first husband, may he rest in peace.

the merchant the wealthiest man in Chelm? Wouldn't his Passover feast be the most sumptuous?

And it was. She arrived well before sunset to find that all the work in the kitchen was done. Of course, Shoshana had Ramunya the servant to help her! The table setting was beautiful. There were seven forks, three knives, and fourteen spoons. Mrs. Chaipul was at a loss to know where to begin.

She sat across the table from Rabbi Kibbitz, who had kind and intelligent blue eyes that twinkled at her, but he never spoke to her in public.

Still, the *charoses* was tasty, with a hint of fresh orange from the Holy land, and the matzah was Reb Stein the baker's finest *shmura*, baked round and crisp.

Then came the chicken soup with matzah balls, which for Mrs. Chaipul were both a shock and a revelation. The walnut-sized matzah balls floating in the soup gave her pause. Floating matzah balls? She had never seen such a thing. She sighed, exercised her jaw a bit, lifted a knaidel with her spoon, and nibbled.

When you're expecting to bite into a rock and instead your teeth sink into whipped air, it comes as something of a surprise. She sat there with the spoon held in front of her open mouth for quite some time.

"Is everything all right?" Shoshana Cantor asked. "Is there enough salt?"

Mrs. Chaipul realized that she was being rude, and she quickly closed her mouth. Her teeth cut through the matzah ball like a hot knife through butter. She chewed, and in seconds the matzah ball had dissolved as if it had never been.

"Interesting," she said quietly. And then she added, so as not to offend her hostess, "Quite tasty."

It was the same at every house she visited in Chelm. Far from being the stones of affliction, the matzah balls were soft, light, and, above all, easily edible.

By the end of Passover, Mrs. Chaipul was disheartened and confused. Had her family been doing something wrong for so many years? Or were the villagers of Chelm the misguided ones?

She took her concerns to Rabbi Kibbitz. This was in the days before they were married. In fact, it was one of the first private conferences that she and the learned man had in his study. She explained her problem and waited for pearls of wisdom.

He was no help at all. "*Kabalah* I know," he said. "But cooking?" He shrugged. "I eat what's in front of me. Too much, if you ask some of the villagers." Then he laughed and patted his great stomach.

Mrs. Chaipul set the questions aside and went back to her restaurant,

A year passed as if it was an instant, and once again Passover was fast approaching.

This year Mrs. Chaipul was determined to be open for business, not for the Seders, but for every other meal. She knew that most housewives only knew how to prepare matzah so many ways. She had in her possession the Chaipul Pesach Cookbook, which detailed more than fourteen hundred recipes with matzah alone, never mind in combination with potato starch!

Once again she ate the first Seder at the Cantor household, and once again she was polite. This time, however, Reb Cantor noticed her face.

"I understand that your restaurant will be open this year," he said. "Will you be making matzah ball soup?"

Mrs. Chaipul grinned. "Yes, of course. It wouldn't be Passover without the famous Chaipul knaidel. I missed them last year and I thought that I would give them away this year to make up for my mistake."

Reb Cantor's eyes widened. "Again you're giving away free food in a village of Jews?"

"Well," shrugged Mrs. Chaipul. "The matzah balls will be free, but the soup will still cost."

On the second day of Passover, despite the fact that it was pouring down rain, the line for Mrs. Chaipul's restaurant snaked out the door. She sent her customers home, wading back and forth through the muddy streets, to bring their own kosher-for-Passover soup bowls so she wouldn't have to spend the whole day and night washing dishes.

Fortunately she had anticipated the crowd, so she had made six kettles the size of washtubs full of matzah balls. Even so, she wasn't sure there was going to be enough, so she had to set a limit of one per customer, at least until everyone had firsts.

As she ladled soup and a knaidel into each bowl, she repeated what her mother had taught her and said with a smile, "Remember that we were once slaves in Egypt."

The villagers thought this was quaint, although they were puzzled when the matzah ball sank to the bottom of their bowls with a clank.

Then they looked for a place to sit. The counters were full; the tables were packed. Many young men and women were forced to slurp standing up.

The restaurant was crowded elbow to elbow, tighter than the shul on Kol Nidre Eve. Still the villagers felt jolly, no matter that it was cold and wet and bucketing down rain outside. In Mrs. Chaipul's restaurant they were all warm and cozy, glowing with anticipation.

The soup was sweet and savory, rich with the snap of parsnip and perfectly peeled paper-thin slices of carrot. It was, in the words of Rabbi Kibbitz, "Good enough to cure even an uncommon cold."

And then it was time to eat the matzah balls.

These were far bigger than those the villagers had been accustomed to. Instead of the size of walnuts or chicken eggs, Mrs. Chaipul's matzah balls were as large as ripe red apples. It wasn't so easy to get such a large knaidel onto your spoon, especially since it seemed a bit weighty. One child was forced to balance his bowl on his knees and use two hands to lift.

At last came the bite. That first bite, the one that defines a matzah ball, and the matzah ball cook, forever in the mind of the eater.

Ow! It hurt. It wasn't so much hard like a rock, but it certainly was dense, like a clay brick before it has set in its mold. Your teeth could dig into it, and it tasted well enough, but it was difficult work, like sawing wood with a nail file.

After two minutes you began to have second thoughts but found that your teeth had sunk in so deeply that they were trapped and there was no choice but to go on. After five minutes your jaws began to ache, and the villagers started to wonder whether Mrs. Chaipul's family had all died of starvation or lockjaw.

At last you bit through with a sudden snap of tooth against tooth and were struck by the realization that you still had to chew the whole bite up because it would be messy and rude to spit it out onto the floor.

So chew it you did. The flavor was good, robust, but it went on and on and on. You nodded and smiled at the neighbor whose face was not six inches from your own. And then you nodded and chewed and smiled some more.

The afternoon dragged into evening, the rain was still pouring, and still they were chewing.

All of a sudden young Doodle, the village orphan, burst into the restaurant. He had forgotten that there was free food and had been wandering through the village looking for someone to tell his news.

"Mrs. Chaipul! Rabbi Kibbitz! The dam on the Bug River has burst! A flood is coming."

There wasn't time to think or plan. A stampede raced out of the restaurant, through the village square, and to the banks of the river where the high water levee they built and maintained every year was threatening to collapse.

A wall of water was about to come rushing toward them. In minutes, Chelm would be washed away and drowned, forgotten in a deluge like the village that Noah and his ark had floated away from.

No one could speak, partly because they were in shock and partly because they were all still chewing. The villagers were so upset, that they hadn't even bothered to put down their bowls and spoons.

Mrs. Chaipul, who had been too busy serving to eat a bite, broke the silence with a command.

"Throw your matzah balls into the river," she shouted. "Aim upstream from the cracks in the levee!"

The villagers did as they were told. Matzah balls went flying. They were caught by the current and washed into the crevasse where they became lodged and stuck fast. More and more matzah balls flew into the river, landing with loud sploshes until the gaps in the wall were sealed tightly and not another dribble leaked through.

The villagers wanted to sigh, but first they had to swallow, which they did, just as the rain stopped and the setting sun emerged from behind a cloud.

And then they cheered: "Mazel Tov for Mrs. Chaipul's famous knaidlach!"

Mrs. Chaipul beamed and kvelled.

Then, much to her surprise, Rabbi Kibbitz kissed her on the cheek.

His beard was surprisingly soft.

He whispered into her ear, "Delicious. You are an amazing woman. You should never change that recipe."

What could she do? She didn't.

Chapter Nine

Chelm Soup

"Something about this soup is not quite right," said Rabbi Yohon Abrahms, the *mashgiach* and head of the yeshiva. He slurped loudly. "Yes, something is not quite right."

Mrs. Chaipul stared at him. "Every day you come into my restaurant," she said. "Every day you order the chicken soup. And every day you say the same thing." She tugged on a pretend beard and made her voice sound just like the schoolteacher's. "'Something about this soup is not quite right.'"

"Well," Rabbi Abrahms shrugged. "It's true."

Reb Cantor, the merchant snickered.

"Don't you start," Mrs. Chaipul pointed a finger. "I haven't been sleeping well. This from you I don't need."

Reb Cantor raised his hands in mock surrender.

"Tell me something, Yohon." Mrs. Chaipul turned her attention to the young rabbi. "No one else seems to have a problem with my soup. If something is so wrong with my soup, why do you come back here every day and order it?"

"Because," Rabbi Abrahms said, "this is the only restaurant in Chelm."

"That's it!" Mrs. Chaipul snapped. "You don't like my soup, you make it yourself." She untied her apron, folded it neatly and then threw it down on the counter in a heap. Then she stormed out of her restaurant and slammed the door behind her.

Both Rabbi Abrahms and Reb Cantor stared at the quivering door.

"But, I don't know how to make soup," the rabbi said quietly.

• • •

A moment later, Mrs. Chaipul stormed into her husband's study.

"I'm sick of it," she shouted. "Sick sick sick sick!" She collapsed in a chair, and burst into tears as if she was slicing a thousand onions.

Rabbi Kibbitz, who was both chief Rabbi of Chelm and Mrs. Chaipul's husband, rose from his chair.

"Chanaleh," he said, "what is wrong? Are you sick?"

"I am not sick."

"You said you were sick."

"I'm not sick."

"Is someone else sick?"

"Oh, you wouldn't understand!" she moaned, burying her head in her hands. "No one likes my cooking. They only come to my restaurant because there are no other restaurants in Chelm."

"I like your cooking," Rabbi Kibbitz said. He patted his wife's head, and tried not to shudder at the memory of the dreadful Chanukah latkes she still cooked just for him. "Especially your latkes."

With that Mrs. Chaipul cried even louder.

"What?" her husband said. "What did I say?"

"You've obviously got no sense of taste," she said. "You couldn't tell the difference between a pickled herring and a pickled shoe."

After that, she was inconsolable. No matter how hard he tried to soothe her, she remained vehemently tearful and distraught.

While Mrs. Chaipul took to her tear-filled bed, Chelm had a problem. Where could everyone go out to eat?

For more than twenty years, Mrs. Chaipul had run her restaurant. Six days a week, she had made a new pot of chicken soup, a batch of chopped liver, roasted a brisket, and so on. Her *knishes* were famous throughout the countryside. Three meals a day she'd served: breakfast for the farm workers, lunch for the marketplace shoppers, and dinner for bachelors and anyone else who wanted to celebrate with a night freed from the drudgery of cooking and cleaning up.

Suddenly, the villagers of Chelm found that the kitchen was closed, the dining room was dark, and the knishes lived only as a fond memory.

Every day for a week a stream of visitors begged Mrs. Chaipul to return to her restaurant, and every day for a week they heard the same answer.

"You don't like my cooking," she cried. "You make it yourself."

"We like your cooking! It's Rabbi Abrahms who's got the problem."

But Mrs. Chaipul was deaf to their pleas.

At last, a delegation visited Rabbi Kibbitz. They set the matter before him, but he shook his head with firm resolve.

"Not this time," Rabbi Kibbitz said. "The last time I put my foot in my mouth, I slept under the kitchen table." He looked at Rabbi Yohon Abrahms. "You started this *mishugas.* You fix it."

All eyes turned to the yeshiva master.

“All right,” said the young Rabbi. “I’ll cook breakfast, teach some classes, do lunch, teach some more, and then make dinner. How difficult could running a restaurant be?”

There was a profound silence in the senior Rabbi’s study, but that did not discourage the young man.

The very next morning, Rabbi Abrahms opened the door to Mrs. Chaipul’s restaurant, tied on her apron, and filled her largest cook pot with water. “Now what?” he wondered. A chicken? Some onions? Hmm, they were very papery. Well, he thought, if paper is good enough for holy prayer books, it’s good enough for soup. And he dropped five whole unpeeled unwashed onions into the kettle.

The next instant, a dozen farm workers walked in the front door and demanded their eggs and challah toast. From that moment on, Rabbi Abrahms was busier than a harried bride preparing her first *Seder* for her new mother-in-law.

Four hours later, several students from the yeshiva wandered into the kitchen looking for their teacher, but he was nowhere to be seen. On the stove, the pot of soup was boiling over, and smoke was pouring from the oven. They heard a pounding sound from the ice room in back, where Mrs. Chaipul kept her meats and vegetables. Quickly, the students opened the ice room door, and out popped Rabbi Abrahms, his fingers blue and with frost crystallized in his beard.

Classes were canceled and by mid-afternoon the restaurant was crowded with regular customers who were pitching in to help the poor foolish young rabbi. They swept the floor, they cleaned the oven, they peeled the potatoes, and they helped with the soup.

Every single man and woman in Chelm had an opinion about chicken soup. This one liked salt, that one liked pepper, another believed that vinegar helped to leech the marrow from the bones. The tailor liked garlic, the butcher preferred onions, and the baker said that a proper soup needed plenty of mushrooms. All of them had their way. There was no stopping them. After all, every one in Chelm knew that Rabbi Abrahms couldn't make soup to save his own life.

One by one, everyone came into the restaurant and took a sip of the soup, they made a face and said, "You know, there is something not quite right about this soup." Then they reached for the paprika or the ginger and made a little correction.

• • •

Just before dinner, Chanah Chaipul noticed that Chelm had grown very quiet. It wasn't Friday night, nor a holiday. Usually there was bustle and hustle outside her bedroom window while villagers hurried to and from the market.

She called for her husband, but he didn't answer. At last, she rose from her bed, stretched, got dressed and went out to see what was what.

When she reached the main square and saw the crowd bulging out the door of her restaurant, she was sure someone had died.

Quickly Mrs. Chaipul pushed her way inside. "What's going on?" she said, her voice filled with concern.

The crowd parted and made a path for her into the kitchen.

There she found Rabbi Abrahms stirring the soup pot. "How is it?"

The rabbi's face paled and he shuddered violently. "Something about this soup is not quite right."

Without a second's hesitation, Mrs. Chaipul picked up a wooden spoon, dipped it into the broth, and took a sip.

At first her mouth puckered as if she'd bitten into the sourest of lemons. It was saltier than the Dead Sea, and as flavorful as dirt. Bleah! She would have spat it out immediately, but she was raised to be polite. (Besides, it was her kitchen and she'd only have to clean up the mess…) At last, her eyes bulged and began to water. Her cheeks flushed red, her nose began to run, and her entire body shivered and shook as she swallowed.

"Oy!" Mrs. Chaipul shouted. "That's awful! Bleah. How many cooks?"

Rabbi Abrahms winced. "All of them."

Mrs. Chaipul looked over her shoulder and saw the mass of villagers, all smiling and wincing with sheepish embarrassment.

"Everyone out!" she shouted. "Come back in an hour."

The restaurant quickly cleared.

Fifty-five minutes later, a long line had formed. Everyone in Chelm waited patiently with their bowl and spoon. At the stroke of six o'clock, the door to the restaurant opened. The line moved quickly, and soon the square was filled with sounds of loud slurping.

At last, Mrs. Chaipul emerged into the twilight.

She found Rabbi Abrahms and Reb Cantor sitting on a bench, sipping soup.

"Well?" said Mrs. Chaipul, her hands on her hips.

Reb Cantor glanced at Rabbi Abrahms with a look of concern.

"You know," said Rabbi Abrahms thoughtfully, "something about this soup is quite… delicious."

Mrs. Chaipul's stone face broadened into a soft smile. A cheer arose.

And from that day until this, six days a week, rain or shine, Mrs. Chaipul's restaurant is open.

Chapter Ten

Sabbath Sickness

Speaking of sickness... Rabbi Kibbitz was sick of Shabbos. He was tired of lighting the candles, eating the meal, leading the services, saying the prayers, studying the Torah and resting resting resting resting.

Intellectually, he understood, that a day of rest was a good idea. Even if the Almighty hadn't mandated it, taking time off from the never-ending grind of work and struggle and survival could be useful and helpful. If you rode a horse too long, it would become lame. Every year the leaves fell from the trees and the Black Forest slumbered only to be reawakened in the spring. Even chickens took breaks from laying egg from time to time. But those were not divinely mandated weekly events. They happened naturally, when needed.

But Rabbi Kibbitz was the chief rabbi of Chelm, which effectively turned the day of rest into a day of work, whether he liked it or not. Unless he was deathly ill, he was expected to show up at the synagogue, to lead the prayers, to encourage the study and to finish the Sabbath with *Havdalah*. For years, he had pretended that these activities weren't really part of the job, that they were things that he liked to do, but...

For a long time, he'd been feeling tired of the ordeal. In theory, the day of the Sabbath was his day off, but the truth was that he had just as many duties as he did during the week, perhaps even more. He was expected to teach at the Yeshiva if Rabbi Abrahms, the school teacher, was unavailable and to be on-call for any sick visits or other needs of the community.

Lying in bed, Rabbi Kibbitz found himself dreading and resenting the coming sunset.

"Are you sick?" came his wife's voice from the kitchen.

For a moment he thought about lying, or just ignoring her and pretending to be asleep, but then Chanah would assume he really was ill, fix up a batch of chicken soup and make him stay in bed all day. It wasn't that he was tired or weary, so much as tired of Shabbos.

"No," he said. "I'm thinking."

"Well, think somewhere else. I have to strip the bed and wash the sheets so we'll have nice clean linens for the Sabbath."

The old rabbi rolled his eyes. Everyone in Chelm, everyone in the Jewish world for that matter, was driven by this cycle of work-work-work-work-work-work, and quick now rest! It made you crazy.

Just last week, he had been enjoying a late afternoon stroll, when he'd been knocked over by Reb Cantor the merchant, who apologized and explained that he was running home to complete some business before sunset. A moment after that, the tailor had knocked him over again, explaining he had a suit to finish before sunset. Finally, just as he was about to go into her restaurant, his wife raced out, and knocked him down for a third time. She hadn't even stopped, but shouted over her shoulder that she had to hurry home to prepare the cholent before the sunset.

The poor rabbi had picked himself off the dirt and dusted himself off. He wasn't hurt. He wasn't even offended. But it made him realize how tired he was of the whole thing.

He was in mid-sigh when Chanah came into the bedroom and yanked the pillow out from under him. His head hit the mattress with a jolt.

"What?" she said, with an impish grin. "You said you were awake and getting up."

He tried to smile, but the best he could manage was a grimace. Nevertheless, he rose, dressed and made his way into the kitchen where his tea, bagel and cream cheese were waiting.

"You seem to be moving slow," Chanah said, "so I made you some extra strong tea. Enjoy."

"I don't want to do Sabbath," he said, softly.

"What?" she said. Sometimes she could be hard of hearing, and sometimes she pretended not to hear to make sure she heard him right.

"I don't want to do Sabbath today," he said. "I'm sick of the whole thing."

His wife pursed her lips. She stood very still and very quiet for a long time.

He was just about to sigh and concede that, all right, he would do his job and stop kvetching, when she put a hand on his shoulder.

"So don't," she said.

"Don't what?" he said.

"Don't. Don't do this Sabbath."

"It's a commandment," the rabbi said.

She shrugged. "You'll atone and you'll be forgiven. I'll get Rabbi Abrahms to do your job tonight."

"It's not supposed to be a job to lead the congregation on the Sabbath. It's supposed to be a privilege."

"Okay," she agreed, "I'll give him your privilege. He'll probably jump at the chance. I'm sure he's got at least one sermon ready to go."

The old rabbi smiled. If he knew his friend, the school teacher had a whole book of sermons written and ready to go..."

"But what will I do?" he asked.

His wife kissed him on the forehead. "Whatever you like."

• • •

Rabbi Kibbitz went to his study, as was his habit, and spent the morning poring over letters and correspondence. At lunch, he tottered out of the synagogue, across the round village square to his wife's restaurant, where he ate his usual meal of extra-lean corned beef on rye with potato salad and a pickle. He lingered over tea for a bit, returned to the study, set some letters out for delivery, and meandered back to his house for a nap.

He lay in bed and waited for sleep to come, but suddenly he wasn't particularly tired. Usually, he would have spent the morning working on his sermon, and his napping dreams would help confirm which parts of the talk to emphasize and which parts to let go.

At lunch, Chanah had told him that she'd already spoken to Rabbi Abrahms about covering the service, and that the young man was thrilled. There was no urgency about anything, including sleep.

So, he got up, pulled on his boots and his coat, and headed out for a walk.

It was a warm day for winter in Chelm, which meant that, while the streets of the village were busy with the bustle before Sabbath, you didn't need to run to prevent frostbite. From time to time, the Rabbi dodged out of the way to avoid getting knocked down, but he found himself enjoying the calm he was feeling.

He almost didn't notice as Little Doodle, the village orphan, fell in step with him, and began to chat about this and that as they strolled out of the village.

Rabbi Kibbitz wondered whether his wife had sent the young boy along to keep an eye on her husband, but decided that it didn't matter. He was enjoying the walk and the talk.

The road to Smyrna meandered between two hills before it cut into the Black Forest, and rather than continuing on or turning around, Rabbi Kibbitz and Doodle made their way up the West Hill, which was also known as Sunset.

At the top, the rabbi was panting, so Doodle steadied him and led him to one of the four logs that were arranged in a square for sitting. From time to time, families had picnics up there.

The sun was just going down. It was a magnificent spectacle. Rabbi Kibbitz couldn't remember the last time he'd been outside at sunset, let alone on top of the best vantage point in Chelm.

The light had a flavor he couldn't remember ever having seen. It was beyond golden because it didn't reflect, so much as shine and illuminate. The leafless branches of all the trees in the Schvartzvald were black but shimmering as if vibrating from the fading light.

For years, Rabbi Kibbitz had noticed that his eyes were beginning to fail. Glasses didn't help much. In the dim candlelight of his study, he'd found himself getting closer and closer to the parchment until his nose was almost touching the scrolls and books as he read.

But sitting outside, none of this bothered him.

As dusk spread its way across the land, he noticed the blurring, but it didn't seem to matter because the splashes of color, as the gold turned to pink and purple, were like great swirling spills of vibrant paints, reaching and turning and transforming.

And then the domed halo of the sun dropped out of sight, and the stars came out.

Maybe it was a distortion of the atmosphere, or a trick of his old eyes, but for some reason, Rabbi Kibbitz saw more stars in the sky than he had seen in decades.

He found tears rolling down his cheeks, and he smiled when Doodle handled him a dry handkerchief.

"Thank you," he said. "I think we should go before it gets too dark to see."

But the path down the hill was illuminated by the stars, and the road from Smyrna was as clearly lit as if it had been daylight.

The village of Chelm was quiet and the streets were empty. For a moment, this confused the rabbi, but then he smiled and remembered it was the Sabbath and they would all be in the Synagogue or at home preparing the meal.

The air felt crisp and clear, and there was no rush to do anything.

He turned to mention this to Doodle, but found that the young boy had gone. Probably off to shul.

The rabbi meandered around the village of Chelm, meeting no one and thinking of nothing. Almost automatically he found himself standing in front of the door to the synagogue. He could go to his house or go back into the woods or...

He could go in.

For a moment he considered.

Was he feeling lonely?

No, not particularly. Did he feel compelled, whether by commandment or shame? Not at all. He was curious, and that thought brought a chuckle to his chest.

He pulled the door open and stepped inside.

Deep in *davening*, no one turned to look. Rabbi Kibbitz hung his coat on a hook, found a spot in the back, and began to sing his prayers. It was strange at first, because he found himself leaping ahead to what page was supposed to come next, and whether to speed things up or to slow them down, but for once that was out of his control, and he found himself simply following along with the flow of the service.

When Rabbi Abrahms gave his D'var Torah talk, Rabbi Kibbitz was pleased that it was both short and profound.[¶]

After the final song was sung, Rabbi Kibbitz found himself shaking hands with Reb Cantor and Reb Stein, and after bundling up warm, walked beside them, until they went to their

---

¶ Though when he considered it later, the old rabbi realized that he couldn't remember a word of the younger rabbi's sermon.

houses and he to his.

He opened the door to the rich smell of roast chicken and matzah ball soup.

"You're early," his wife said. "Though I suppose not. Are you hungry?"

"Famished," he said, as he washed his hands. But before he sat down at the table, he took his wife in his arms and danced her around the room until they were both quite flushed.

He told her about his day, and she talked about hers.

When he told her that he hoped she wouldn't be too upset, but he had decided to let Rabbi Abrahms lead most, if not all, of the Sabbath services from now on, she leaned over and kissed his cheek.

"It's about time," she laughed.

Well, Rabbi Kibbitz thought. I wonder what will come next.

The chicken was delicious and tender, the soup was heavenly, and the matzah balls were, as usual, as solid as rocks.

Chapter Eleven

The End?

"You don't love me any more."

Rabbi Kibbitz looked up from his reading. "What?"

"I said, you don't love me any more." Chanah Chaipul's face was somber. It was a statement of fact.

It was early in the morning. Every day, the two of them got up just before dawn. The rabbi prayed, while his wife made breakfast. Then they sat down at the table and ate before she hurried off to her restaurant. Usually the meal was quiet. They'd been married for years now, and there wasn't that much new to say.

Rabbi Kibbitz looked at his wife, puzzled. "How can you say that? It's not true. I tell you that I love you every day."

"That's what you say."

"I brought you flowers last week."

"They were very nice. Thank you so much." She nodded her head, rose from the table, and began folding her apron.

Was she serious? he wondered. "Chanah," he asked, "did something happen?"

She stopped, thought a moment, and then shook her head. "No. Nothing happened. In fact, that's part of the problem. Nothing ever happens. Day in and day out it's all the same. I cook the meals here, I cook the meals at the restaurant. You pray here, you pray at the shul. We say hello to each other and go to sleep. Animals have more passion in their days."

"Well, that's why they're animals."

She stared at him with contempt, and he knew he'd said something stupid. He could try to rescue it with an apt quotation from the Torah, but somehow he didn't think that would help.

"Perhaps," he suggested, "I could take you out to dinner."

"Where? I run the only restaurant in Chelm. It would take us half a day to walk to Smyrna. I'd have to close the restaurant. We'd eat a lousy dinner, spend too much money, and then walk home in the dark. No thank you."

"I could hire a carriage."

She rolled her eyes. "More money down the drain. No. It's too late. Maybe last week if you'd surprised me, but now... You're only doing it because you know I'm upset."

"So, is there a better reason?"

"Yes," she snapped. "Because you want to. Because you love me."

"But I do love you!"

Again she rolled her eyes. "You know, we don't have children. We don't have to stay together."

The rabbi's jaw dropped. "What are you talking about?"

"I think you know what I'm talking about."

"It's nonsense!" His voice rose to a shout. "Utter nonsense."

"So, do you have to yell? I don't think it's nonsense. My restaurant is nonsense! I have to go now and open up. The farmers will be hungry. If you're here this evening, we'll discuss it some more."

"What do you mean, if?"

But it was too late. She'd gone.

All day Rabbi Kibbitz was in a fuddle. He couldn't make head or tails of it. His marriage to Chanah was like a pair of comfortable shoes, a perfect fit. And shoes didn't just disintegrate like that. First you saw rips, a certain thinness in the sole... True, they hadn't been talking much recently. But the years were flying by. They were both too old for children, and perhaps that was the problem. Had they married too late in their lives? Should he have asked her sooner? It was foolish to speculate, but he couldn't help himself. Now that he thought about it, he had detected a certain coolness in her voice, and she had recently developed a habit of dropping his dinner plate on the table and telling him to get his fork and knife himself... Why hadn't the flowers worked?

He didn't dare go to the restaurant for lunch, as was his habit. When it came time to teach his afternoon Torah class to the yeshiva students, he felt faint. He was too old for this nonsense. He was the senior rabbi of Chelm, respected by all. All except his wife. Everything he'd said this morning she'd found fault with. Why? Because she thought he didn't love her.

And she didn't want him to come home. That was clear. She'd said so.

What would happen if he went home? She'd throw his plate on the table, tell him to get his own fork and knife, and then she would tell him again that he didn't love her. He'd say that he did. Then he'd try and prove it.

Was love something you could prove with logic? He didn't think so. So how was he going to explain to her that she was wrong? He loved her deeply, but he couldn't prove it. He couldn't explain it.

Fine. So be it.

After the evening service, instead of going home, the rabbi sat behind his desk, and read and thought, absorbing himself in the wisdom of the ages, until at last his beard fell into his lap, his cheek rested on the book, and loud snores filled his study.

Within two days, everyone in Chelm knew that the marriage was falling apart like an overcooked brisket.

In the marketplace the gossips talked of nothing else.

"I knew it wouldn't last," said the first *yenta.*

"What do you mean," said another, "for twenty-five years it's lasted."

"He never should have let her keep her name."

"And she works, too," added a third. "What kind of a rabbi lets his wife work?"

"I for one am glad that the restaurant is still around," said the second.

"But he never stands up to her. In everything else he's a man of authority. With her he's as spineless as an egg."

Everyone stared.

"Eggs don't have spines," the third yenta said.

"My point exactly."

With that, they all fell into a puzzled silence. One by one, they gathered their purchases and went home.

For a week, Chanah Chaipul kept to the old routine. She rose in the morning and fixed breakfast for two. Then she threw his out. Then she worked all day at the restaurant, coming home only just in time for dinner. She set two places at the table and waited until the food was nearly cold. Then she ate her meal, and wrapped the other for him. Before bed, she sent a boy with the food to the synagogue so that the poor man wouldn't starve to death, but other than that she didn't care. On the Sabbath, she sat in the women's balcony of the shul, and ignored the whispers and stares. For a week she did this, and then she gave up.

How could I let this happen to me? she wondered as she caught herself about to ask his empty chair to pass the salt. I used to be so strong and independent. Now my mind is going and I have an empty place in my heart.

That night she cried herself to sleep, and the next morning had not a single kind word for any customer in her restaurant.

Perhaps it would have been different if she had known that he too cried. One morning, a little boy asked the rabbi why he was hanging so many books up to dry. "A leak in the roof," he said, hoarsely.

Everyone in Chelm was worried. Usually when a couple had marital problems the man went to the rabbi and the woman went to Mrs. Chaipul. Inevitably it all worked out. Obviously, this wasn't going to happen.

One afternoon, there was a knock at the door of the rabbi's study.

He looked up, and was surprised to see his wife standing there. Usually she just barged right in.

He looked down and pretended to finish the page he had been reading. It took a while, and he didn't remember a word. At last, he looked up again. "Come in," he said, beckoning.

She hesitated, entered, and sat. She didn't say a word.

"So, Mrs. Chaipul," he said, "what can I do for you?"

"Rabbi..." She opened her mouth and then made a face. "What is that smell? Is that you? You haven't been washing have you?"

He smiled and lied. "I was enjoying a particularly ripe piece of cheese this morning. Would you like a taste?"

She shuddered. He looked awful. Thin and haggard, and very very old.

For his part, the rabbi was doing his best to keep his eyes on his wife's face, because if he let his gaze drift, he found himself thinking that even after all these years she looked more beautiful than ever.

He smiled. The words, "I love you so much," were on the tip of his tongue when she spoke.

"I want a *get*."

His heart sank. A get? A divorce? She doesn't want me? Why? What did I do? Nothing. But she wants one... All right, fine.

What he said was, "Tell me what the reason is, please. As the rabbi, I need to follow certain formalities..."

"Desertion," she said. "My husband has moved out of our house."

"What!" He was stunned. "Didn't you ask him to? That's what he thought."

"He was wrong," she said. "If he'd bothered to talk with me, I would have told him so."

"You could have sent him a note."

"So could he!"

"Calm down." The rabbi raised his hand. "Please, let me ask you a question. Do you love him?"

He put his hands on his lap, and, even though it was a Christian superstition, crossed his fingers.

She paused. And then said, "I don't know if I can love someone who I don't know."

He shook his head. "I'm not following you. You've been married for a long time, you knew him for a long time before that. And just the other day, you were complaining that you knew him only too well!"

"Are you going to listen?"

He nodded. "I'm listening."

"It's foolish," she said.

"Mrs. Chaipul," he said, "this is Chelm. At some time in our lives, we are all fools."

She nodded. "This is a big one. I can't believe it's gone on so long."

He waited. She fidgeted. He tried to look understanding. She stared at the ceiling.

At last, she spoke, "I don't know his name."

"What?"

"I don't know my own husband's first name. I know his title. I know his family name. I have called him husband. I have called him nicknames and pet names and from time to time horrible names, but I don't know his first name. I wrote a letter to his friend Rabbi Sarnoff, but he was useless. I tried to look it up on our *ketubah*, but I can't find our ketubah! And as far as I can tell, no one in Chelm knows my husband's first name!"

"You're kidding me. Really? All this for that?"

She burst into tears. "That and the fact is that he doesn't love me any more."

This was too much for the wisest man in Chelm. He could no longer listen objectively. He rose from his chair, walked around his desk, and put his hand on her shoulder.

"But I do love you," he said. "I love you more than I could possibly imagine. When you said you wanted a get, I thought that without you I will have a heart attack and die."

"So then," she sobbed, "why won't you tell me your first name?"

"Who knew you didn't know?" he said. "Chanah. Look at me."

She raised her eyes to him, and he fell in love again. Can you fall in love with someone who you've always loved? He hoped so.

"My name is Samuel," he said.

"But my first husband's name was Samuel."

He nodded. "You can see why I wouldn't want to bring it up all the time. But it wasn't on purpose. I thought you knew."

"Samuel? Sam Kibbitz? Sammy? Sameleh? That's really your name?"

He nodded again. "You should know that I didn't desert you. I thought you wanted me to go. I love you Chanah. I have always loved you. Do you believe me yet?"

"Yes, Sam," she said.

"Do you love me?"

"Oh, yes, Sam."

"Can we forget about this get thing?"

She nodded.

"Can I come home now?"

Again she nodded.

"I have a favor," he said.

"What is it, Sam?"

"Can we keep my name a secret? I had no idea that people didn't know my name. But, since they don't, let's not make an issue of it. It might cause trouble. My name will be yours only. A gift from me to you, so that you will always know that I love you."

"All right," she said. "But on one condition."

"What's that?"

"You have to let me burn those clothes."

They smiled, they laughed, they hugged, and then they went home.

• • •

Two days later, the busybodies were back in the marketplace.

"It's disgusting," said one yenta. "I can't believe it. The two of them? Holding hands in public. Giggling. Acting like teenagers. At their age!"

“I don’t know,” said a second gossip. “I think it’s sweet.”

“Feh.” The third one shuddered. “It makes me nauseous just thinking about it.”

The End

Afterword

Most of *The Village Life Series* can be read in any order. Time is not always linear, and stories often overlap. This may lead to some confusion. Which is natural, given the nature of Chelm.

Halfway through writing the novel, **The Village Twins**, I realized that Rabbi Kibbitz and Mrs. Chaipul had somehow gotten married, but I couldn't interrupt the adventures of Abraham and Adam Schlemiel to explain it.

Fortunately for everyone's sanity, she insisted on keeping her name. But then she and the rabbi demanded their story be told.

A Village Romance was like assembling a jigsaw puzzle without any edges. For me, compiling a collection usually changes the stories. The first published version of "Why the Bride and Groom are on the Wedding Cake" made no mention of Mrs. Chaipul, but of course she must have been there. And it wasn't until the last pages of "The End?" that Rabbi Kibbitz's first name was finally revealed.

Some chapters made sense in several places.

The Village Feasts balanced the humor of "Mrs. Chaipul's Lead Sinker Matzah Balls" against the Passover struggles of Reb Stein, the Baker, and the Gold family's fortunes.

Winter Blessings features gifts from the Schlemiels and Golds, but it wouldn't be the same without "The Lethal Latkes" and "A Chanukah Surprise."

If you read this book first, I hope you'll enjoy revisiting slightly different versions of these stories surrounded by similar tales. If you began with one of the others, I hope you said, "Ah ha!"

As Rabbi Kibbitz says at dinner, "The kasha is good. The gravy is good. Together they are delicious."

To which Mrs. Chaipul answers, "If you want more, just ask."

– *Izzy Abrahmson, Providence*

Glossary

Chelm: *Chelm* is a village known for it's "wise" people, who are frequently foolish. Pronounce it like you've got something stuck in your throat, "Chh-elm."

chelmener: The people who live in Chelm.

challah: A delicious braided bread made with eggs. At Rosh Hashonah, challahs (the plural is really *challot*) are round, signifying a year coming full circle.

Chanukah/Hanukkah: The festival of lights. Several spellings.

charoses: A tasty blend of chopped or mashed fruits and nuts, eaten at Passover

chupah: The wedding canopy, often cloth, supported with four poles.

davening: A style of praying bobbing back and forth. Keeps you limber.

dreidel: A four-sided top for a Chanukah game.

get: A divorce paper.

goyishe: Someone or something that's not Jewish.

harey: Part of the wedding vows. Just before groom places the ring on the bride's finger.

Havdalah: The closing of the Sabbath. Beautiful.

hora: A vigorous circle dance. Lots of fun!

Kabalah: Jewish numerology. Magic, maybe? Shhh. It's secret.

ketubah: The wedding contract.

kinder: Children. They're cute. Mostly.

klezmer: Jewish jazz. Hot stuff.

knish: Dough stuffed with meat or potatoes. Sort of a Jewish calzone.

kreplach: A noodle-dumpling. Think of it as a Jewish wonton, but never fried. And sometimes filled with cabbage…

kugel: An incredibly rich pudding. Often made with noodles. Mmmm.

kvetch: 1) To complain. 2) A complaint. 3) The complainer.

latke: A pancake fried in oil. At Passover, latkes are made with matzah meal. At Hanukkah they are made with potatoes.

matzah/matzoh/matzo/matza: Unleavened bread for Passover. Bland. Dry. Tasteless. Did we mention dry? Spell it however you like.

matzah ball: A dumpling made from matzah meal and egg. The best float in soup. Mrs. Chaipul's are so heavy they make dents on the bottom of the bowl.

Mashgiach: The rabbi in charge of making sure everything's kosher.

Mazel Tov! Good luck! Usually shouted.

mishugas: Craziness.

mitzvah: A good deed. Not to be confused with a bar mitzvah.

oy: An expression of excitement and often pain. "Oy! My back!" or "Oy, I can't believe you're wearing that to a wedding!"

Passover/Pesach: The celebration of the Israelites' exodus from Egypt. Celebrated for eight days in the diaspora or seven days, depending on where you live and what you believe.

Rabbi: A teacher. Often the leader of a synagogue's congregation.

Reb: A wise man. And, since everyone in Chelm is wise, the men are all called Reb... as in Reb Stein, Reb Cantor, and so on. (Yes, of course there are wise women in Chelm! But they don't brag.)

Rebbe: A rabbi, but a smidge wiser.

Rebbetzin: The rabbi's wife.

Rosh Hashanah: The Jewish New Year.

Shabbas / Shabbos / Shabbat
The Jewish Sabbath. Starts Friday night at sunset. Ends Saturday at sunset.

shmura: An extra-special matzah, eaten during Passover.

shul: A synagogue.

shvitz: To perspire.

schmaltz: Chicken fat, used for cooking. Yummy, even if it does cause heart attacks.

svelte: Slender and elegant, but not too skinny.

Smyrna: Another village. Near Chelm.

Torah: The Five Books of Moses. The first five books of the Hebrew Bible, which is frequently called the Old Testament.

yeshiva: The religious school.

yenta: A gossip, a busybody, someone whose nose is in everybody else's business.

Yom Kippur: The Day of Atonement. Pray all day. No food.

zaftig: Rubenesque, healthily and beautifully plump.

About the Author

Izzy Abrahmson is the pen name for Mark Binder, a professional storyteller, and the author of more than two dozen books and audio books for families and adults. He has toured the world delighting readers and listeners of all ages with his stories, interspersed with his unique klezmer harmonica sounds.

Under his "real" name, Mark began writing about The Village as the editor of *The Rhode Island Jewish Herald*. These stories were so popular that they have been published in newspapers and magazines around the world. His epic *Loki Ragnarok* was nominated for an Audie Audiobook Award for Best Original Work, and *Transmit Joy* won a Parents' Choice Gold Award for Audio Storytelling. Mark is also a playwright, and the founder of the American Story Theater. In his spare time he bakes bread and makes pizza. He lives in Providence with his wife, who is a brilliant ceramic artist.

For tour dates, news, and bonus material visit:
izzyabe.com or **markbinderbooks.com**

Keep Reading

We hope you've enjoyed this book.

May we send you a bonus
Village Life story as a gift?

Visit **izzyabe.com**

Sign up for news and tour dates
And the latest book releases.

Please do consider telling your friends
and writing a review.

You can also tag us on social media
#TheVillageLife
@IzzyAbrahmson

We value your readership.
Have an excellent day.

The Village Life Series

"The Village is snuggled in an indeterminate past that never was but certainly should have been, a past filled with love, humor, adventures and more than occasional misadventures. And when you go, be sure to bring the kids." – *The Times of Israel*

The Village Twins - a novel for adults
When the seventh daughter of a seventh daughter has twins, you know there will be trouble. Abraham and Adam Schlemiel star in this warm comedy that blends ordinary life with adventure and epic confusion.

"In the spirit of Sholem Aleichem… identical twins, confused from birth, will charm with their simplicity and sincerity." – *AudioFile*

A Village Romance - a short and sweet book
He's the wisest man in the village. She runs the only restaurant. They are both widowed…. What could possibly go wrong?

"engaging tales… Village stories that deftly lift a curtain on a world of friendly humor and touching details of Jewish life."
– *Kirkus Reviews*

Winter Blessings
National Jewish Book Award for Family Literature Finalist!
Eleven funny and heart-warming Chanukah stories and a novella.

"Parents and grandparents will enjoy reading selections aloud and retelling the stories." – *AJL Newsletter*

The Village Feasts
Ten tasty Passover tales for adults and children of all ages. Delightful and amusing.

The Council of Wise Women - a novel for adults – Coming Soon!
Another set of twins? Oy! The birth of Rachel and Yakov Cohen bring new blessings and challenges to The Village.

books, ebooks, and audiobooks available at your favorite retailer and at IzzyAbe.com

An excerpt from THE VILLAGE TWINS

"Oy!"

"Push!"

"Jacob, stop that!" Rebecca Schlemiel snapped at her husband. "We're moving a table, not giving birth. Not yet anyway."

"I'm practicing," Jacob laughed. "It's going to happen any day now."

They both looked down at Rebecca's bulging belly. It was huge, the size of a boulder, and just as heavy.

"I can only wish," Rebecca said. She looked around the crowded kitchen and not for the first time wondered how they were going to fit another person into their lives. The house was tiny. In fact, calling it a house at all was a gracious compliment. Two rooms – a bedroom and the kitchen, plus a privy out back. "Do you think the crib is really going to fit between the table and the cupboard?"

"Relax," Jacob said. "I measured it myself. The first knuckle of my thumb is exactly one inch long. The distance between the cupboard and the table is…" He began measuring again.

Rebecca looked at her husband, inching his thumb along the floor, shook her head, and put on a pot of water for tea. This was going to take a while….

Continued in Izzy Abrahmson's full-length novel, THE VILLAGE TWINS

What else do they say about Izzy Abrahmson's Village Life?

"Abrahmson's prose savvily mixes the homey and the surreal, and he's a master...Readers young and old will be delighted..."
– *Publishers Weekly*

"The Village is snuggled in an indeterminate past that never was but certainly should have been, a past filled with love, humor, adventures and more than occasional misadventures. And when you go, be sure to bring the kids."
– *The Times of Israel*

WINTER BLESSINGS...

"...brings together traditional style Jewish storytelling and contemporary Chanukah traditions. The stories are propelled by a cast of entertaining and humorous characters..."
– *AJL News and Reviews*

THE VILLAGE FEASTS...

"...an entertaining comic celebration of Jewish life and tradition.... wryly funny with dollops of heartwarming schmaltz."
– *Kirkus Reviews."*

Great for family reading aloud."
– *Seattle JT News*

"10 silly, charming, whimsical, big-hearted stories"
– *Mark Levenson, author of Hidden Saints*

www.ingramcontent.com/pod-product-compliance
Lightning Source LLC
LaVergne TN
LVHW091010080826
845145LV00003B/1210
* 9 7 8 1 9 4 0 0 6 0 5 3 8 *